W9-AYE-903
34663001078986
Hampstead Public Library
WITHDRAWN
HAMPSTEAD PUBLIC LIBRARY

LYRIC McKERRIGAN, SECRET LIBRARIAN

BY JACOB SAGER WEINSTEIN

ILLUSTRATED BY VERA BROSGOL

CLARION BOOKS
Houghton Mifflin Harcourt
Boston New York

For Joe and Erin –J.S.W.

To the Multnomah County Library –V.B.

Clarion Books
3 Park Avenue
New York, New York 10016

Clarion Books is an imprint of Houghton Mifflin Harcourt Publishing Company.

hmhco.com

The illustrations in this book were done in ink on bristolboard with color in Adobe Photoshop.

Library of Congress Cataloging-in-Publication Data
Names: Sager Weinstein, Jacob, author. | Brosgol, Vera, illustrator.
Title: Lyric McKerrigan, secret librarian / by Jacob Sager Weinstein ; illustrated by Vera Brosgol.
Description: Boston ; New York : Clarion Books, Houghton Mifflin Harcourt, [2018] | Summary: When evil Dr. Glockenspiel threatens all the books in the world, only one person can stop him—a book-wielding, super-secret operative called Lyric McKerrigan.
Identifiers: LCCN 2016046354 | ISBN 9780544801226 (hardcover)
Subjects: | CYAC: Good and evil—Fiction. | Books and reading—Fiction. | Librarians—Fiction. | Spies—Fiction.
Classification: LCC PZ7.1.S245 Lyr 2018 | DDC [E]—dc23
LC record available at https://lccn.loc.gov/2016046354

Manufactured in China
SCP 10 9 8 7 6 5 4 3 2 1
4500711345

WANTED
GLOCKENSPIEL

Doctor Glockenspiel has escaped from his cell.
DEPOSITORY FOR THE CRIMINALLY NAUGHTY

And now, from a secret lair in an Arctic iceberg, he makes his demand:

I WANT ONE BILLION TRILLION DOLLARS, OR MY ARMY OF GIANT MOTHS WILL EAT THE WORLD'S BOOKS!!!

The world sends its
best secret agents.

Doctor Glockenspiel
sends his best henchmen
to capture them.

What will the world do?
WORLD NEWS
REC
OH NO!
Where can we turn for help?
Who loves books so much that she would risk her life to save them?
!

LYRIC
MCKERRIGAN
SECRET
LIBRARIAN!

Every corridor in the iceberg is watched by security cameras.
DISGUISES FOR FUN!
SECURITY
DEFEATING EVIL IN THREE EASY STEPS

Ten thousand cameras, and nothing ever happens! I'm so bored.
Hey. I know how you could pass the time.

Hmm.
JUST SEW STORIES
FIVE CHILDREN & KNIT
MAKE CLAY for DUCKLINGS
But who was that janitor?
Who knew just the right book
to mop away boredom?
JUST SEW STORIES

LYRIC
McKERRIGAN
SECRET
LIBRARIAN!

Where is Lyric McKerrigan, Secret Librarian???
Bring her to me, or I'll string you up by your ears!

I hate it when I get strung up by my ears.
I got strung up by my *toes* yesterday.
Bosses can do anything they want.
BOILER ROOM

You know . . .
I have a book you might find interesting.
FIVE LITTLE MONKEYS JUMP ON THE BOSS
IF YOU GIVE A MOUSE A CONTRACT
WORKER'S
YOUR BOSS CAN'T DO THAT!
LITTLE BOSS ON THE PRAIRIE

But who was that plumber? Who had just the right book in her toolbox?
YOUR BOSS CAN'T DO THAT!
YOUR BOSS CAN'T DO THAT!
LYRIC McKERRIGAN
SECRET LIBRARIAN!

I wish there were some way we could escape this cell.
But how can we? We don't have the key.
Look. The jailer is here with our daily gruel.

HOW
TO
PICK
LOCKS

But who was that jailer? Who served up just the right book at just the right time?

LYRIC McKERRIGAN
SECRET LIBRARIAN!
G

The secret agents surround Doctor Glockenspiel.
Throw your death ray on the ground and put your hands up!

Attack them! Or I'll string you up by your nose hairs!
No! You aren't allowed to string us up by anything!
Plus you're supposed to pay us!
We're going on strike.
YOUR BOSS

THEN I SHALL HAVE MY REVENGE!
I shall destroy every book in the world!

WHIRR
WHIRR
WHIRR
Fly, my pretties, fly!

SKRee!
SKRee!
SKRee!

But then . . . someone shines a flashlight onto a book.

Story time!

. . . says a voice from the shadows.

"Once upon a time, there was a hungry moth. He ate a book. It tasted okay."

"Then he tried some nice wool clothes, and they tasted *fantastic*."

"'Yes, sir,' said the moth. 'Nothing like thick, heavy wool clothes to satisfy my hungry tummy.'"

Doctor Glockenspiel
looks at the moths.
The moths look at
Doctor Glockenspiel.

He doesn't get far.

And now that his plans, like his clothes, are in tatters . . .

. . . who files him away in the Depository for the Criminally Naughty?
MY NEW JAILER AND ME
HONEST IN WONDERLAND
HOW TO WIN FRIENDS & INFLUENCE HENCHMEN
I picked these out for you!
XXX
Lyric

Who saved the world today?
Who will save it again tomorrow?
RETURNED
GOODNIGHT CRIME

SECRET LIBRARIAAAN!
DEPUTY LIBRARIAN

GLOCKENSPIEL
CAUGHT!!